With thanks to the Mountain Bothies Association who maintain these wonderful buildings, but cannot guarantee there are no ghosts!

This is a story about hiker named Bill, who trekked to a bothy far away in the hills.

Now rumour has it there lived a ghost and that noisy visitors were frightened the most.

But Bill did not believe in such tales, as he opened the door and stepped out of the gale.

Removing his boots and taking off his pack, relieving the stress and ache in his back.

For a night in the bothy was what he had hoped, as the last rays of sun shone on the hill slope.

Settling down to take everything in, the visitor book opened, but not by him!

This was unnerving but Bill thought it a draught, not a ghost causing mischief by applying its craft.

The sun had set and now it was dark, a fire needed lighting and for that a spark.

Out of his pack Bill pulled out a flint and on the table he set it next to his drink.

After stacking the fire he got to his feet and noticed his flint had moved onto the seat.

Bill couldn't be sure what he saw in the gloom, so he lit a candle to light the room.

To believe it a ghost felt a little absurd, but he was startled by a sound from the corner he heard.

A shriek like he'd never heard before, so he backed away towards the door.

The noise stopped dead in the cold, then the candle blew out and the dark took hold.

Grabbing his torch that was next to his scotch, he turned it on and looked at his watch.

Midnight approached and outside came the rain, a face looked through the window pane.

The terror sent shivers down Bill's spine, what should he do at 11:59?

He decided his next step was to leave, the ghost could get up to its own mischief.

Bill had suffered such a terrible fright, he packed his belongings and ran into the night.

This is the tale of two small pals, who lived in a bothy far away in the hills.

Not many visited night or day, the bothy was too far away.

Those that arrived did not often stay, the friends wanted quiet, they liked it this way.

It wasn't the damp that made visitors leave, but the ghost of the bothy up to mischief...

The friends had a secret, the ghost was a scam. It was nothing more than just a big plan.

First there was Spider and he was the brains, using his web to defend his domain.

Then there was Mouse who was the muscle and together they pulled off their elaborate hustle.

On a cold windy day at a quarter to four, the bothy door opened and the peace was no more.

A hiker stepped through and removed his pack, moaning loudly as he stretched out his back.

The quiet now gone the friends knew what to do, they sprang into action as if this was their cue.

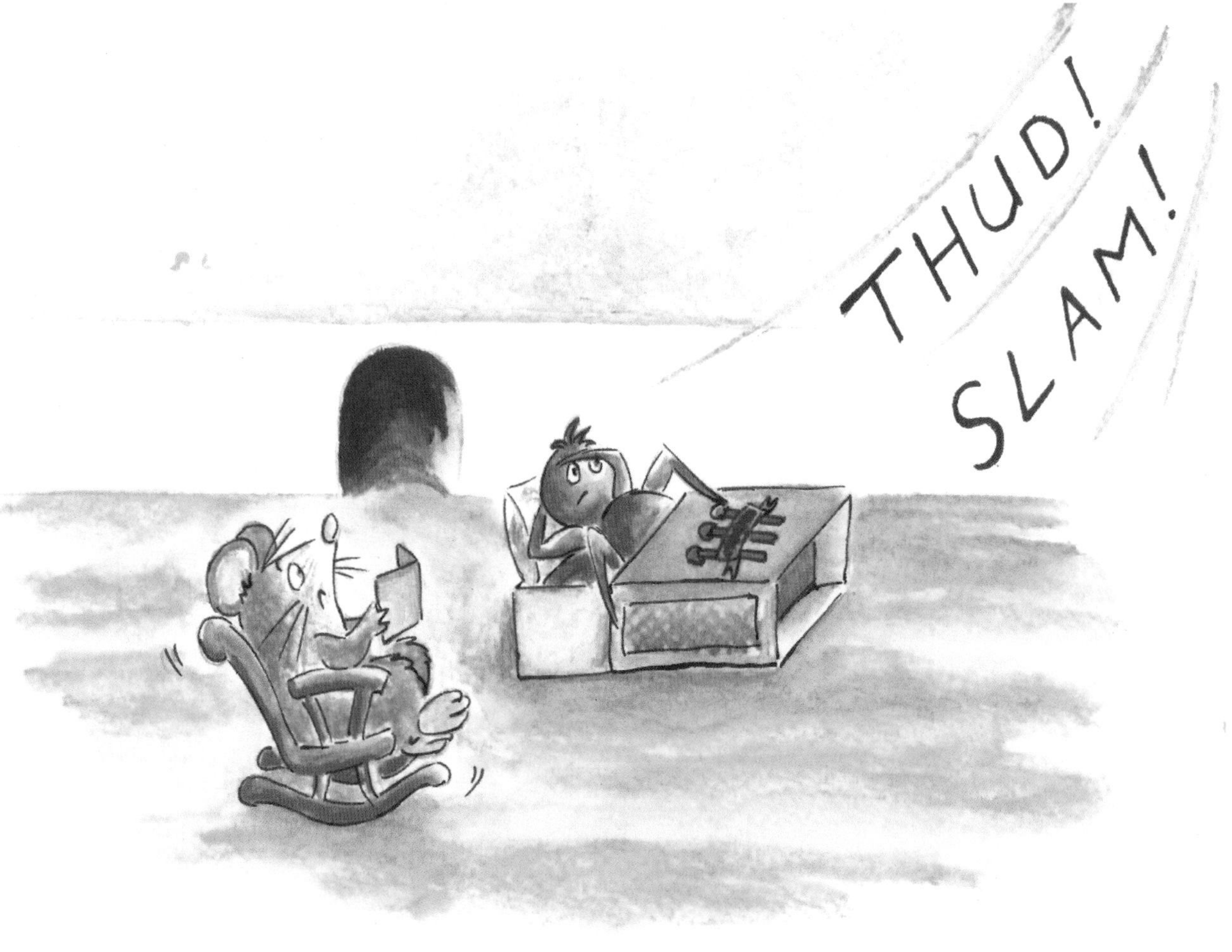
THUD!
SLAM!

The hiker sat down beside the fire, Spider spun a web like a strand of wire.

Attaching an end to the visitor book, he turned a page to make the hiker look.

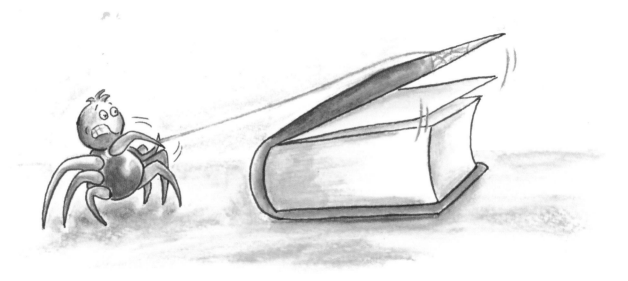

This did not have the desired effect, as the hiker sat still looking perplexed.

Now was the time to step up their game, as the hiker got his flint to produce a flame.

Seeing his chance as the hiker set it down, Mouse scampered across the table not making a sound.

And while the hiker stacked the wood, Mouse pushed the flint as hard as he could.

Off the table and onto the chair, the hiker turned around to stare.

With the hiker trying to light a candle, it was still Mouse who held the mantle.

In the corner of the bothy was a pan with a hole, that Mouse used as a megaphone to achieve his goal.

Squeaking loudly with all his might, the resulting shriek gave the hiker a fright.

This seemed to work as the hiker went pale, Spiders turn again, they were not going to fail.

Dangling from the ceiling there was no doubt, Spider span like a fan and blew the flame out.

Everything dark Spider had to be quick, as he scurried to the window for his next trick.

While the hiker looked for his torch in haste, Spider spun a web in the shape of a face.

The light of the torch catching the web, not a face did he see but a ghost instead.

Their plan had worked as they had thought; the hiker packed his things that he had brought.

And in such a terrible haste, he forgot his bread and meat paste.

Then running out into the night, he'd left the friends a tasty bite.

So they settled down to eat, knowing their plan was now complete.

First published 2018.

ISBN-13: 978-1727688610

ISBN-10: 1727688619

Other titles authored by James Fenwick and illustrated by Duane Nunn.

The Paper Dragon

Printed in Great Britain
by Amazon